# DRAWING ZENTANGLE® BIRDS

## Hannah Geddes

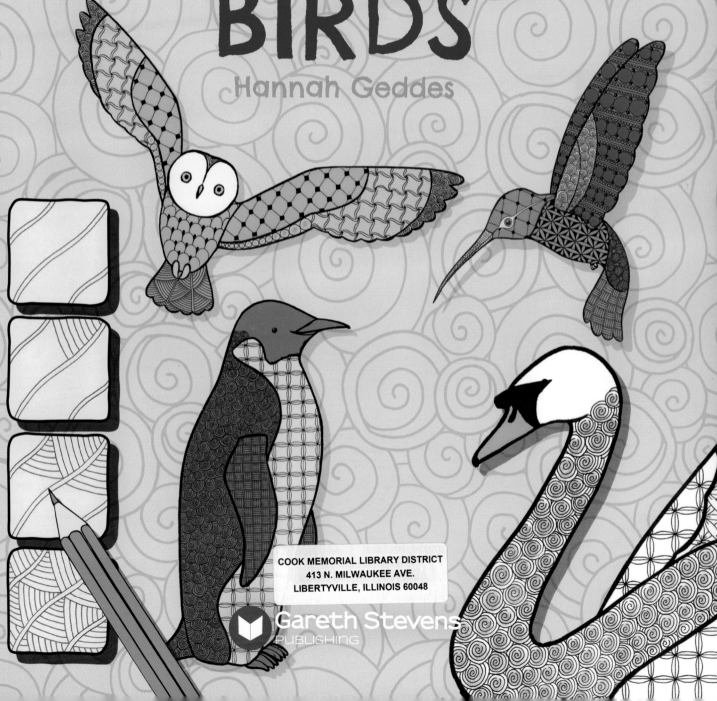

Gareth Stevens
PUBLISHING

## Acknowledgments

The Zentangle® method was created by Rick Roberts and Maria Thomas.

"Zentangle"®, the Zentangle® logo, "Anything is possible one stroke at a time", "Bijou", "Certified Zentangle Teacher"®, "CZT"®, "Zentangle Apprentice"®, and "Zentomology" are trademarks, service marks, or certification marks of Rick Roberts, Maria Thomas, and/or Zentangle Inc.

PERMISSION TO COPY ARTWORKS: The written instructions, designs, patterns, and projects in this book are intended for the personal use of the reader and may be reproduced for that purpose only. Any other use, especially commercial use, is forbidden under law without the written permission of the copyright holder.

All the tangles in this book are Zentangle® originals created by Rick Roberts and Maria Thomas, apart from: Crezn't (page 15) and Gingham (page 16) by Margaret Bremner CZT.

Please visit our website, www.garethstevens.com.
For a free color catalog of all our high-quality books,
call toll free 1-800-542-2595 or fax 1-877-542-2596.

CATALOGING-IN-PUBLICATION DATA

Names: Geddes, Hannah.
Title: Drawing Zentangle® birds / Hannah Geddes.
Description: New York : Gareth Stevens Publishing, 2018. | Series: How to draw Zentangle® art | Includes index.
Identifiers: ISBN 9781538207253 (pbk.) | ISBN 9781538207277 (library bound) | ISBN 9781538207062 (6 pack)
Subjects: LCSH: Drawing--Technique--Juvenile literature. | Repetitive patterns (Decorative arts)--Juvenile literature. |
    Birds in art--Juvenile literature.
Classification: LCC NC730.G43 2018 | DDC 741.201'9--dc23

Published in 2018 by
Gareth Stevens Publishing
111 East 14th Street, Suite 349
New York, NY 10003

Step-outs and Zentangle® Inspired Artworks by Hannah Geddes
Text by Catherine Ard
Outline illustrations by Katy Jackson
Designed by Trudi Webb and Emma Randall
Edited by Frances Evans

Printed in China

CPSIA compliance information: Batch CS17GS: For further information contact
Gareth Stevens, New York, New York at 1-800-542-2595.

# Contents

# Flying High

Zentangle® is a drawing method created by Rick Roberts and Maria Thomas. It teaches you how to create beautiful pieces of art using simple **patterns** called tangles. Tangling is a really fun, relaxing way to get creative, and it brings out the artist in everyone. You can tangle wherever and whenever the mood takes you!

This book takes inspiration from the skies to create Zentangle® Inspired Artworks ("ZIAs"). Each project features a beautiful bird and demonstrates tangles that suit that particular creature. Try our tangles or mix and match them across projects to decorate your own feathered friends.

# Pens and Pencils

Pencils are good for drawing "strings" (page 18) and for adding shade to your tangles. A 01 (0.25-mm) black pen is good for fine lines. Use a 05 (0.45-mm) or 08 (0.50-mm) pen to fill in bigger areas. You can use paints to brighten up your art, too!

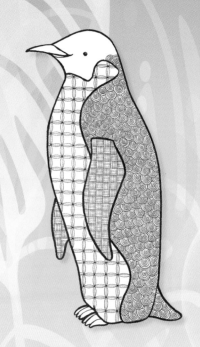

# Paper

Tangles are usually drawn on a square 3.5-inch (9 cm) tile made of thin cardboard. You can use any kind of paper, but if you want to make your tangles really special, use good quality art paper. Have some tracing paper on hand so you can trace the images in this book to use as outlines for your Zentangle® Inspired Artworks.

# Useful Techniques

There are some special techniques you might come across when you tangle. A "highlight" is a gap or blank space in the lines of your tangles. Highlights can make your tangles look shiny!

An "aura" is a line traced around the inside or outside of a shape. Use auras to add a sense of movement to your art.

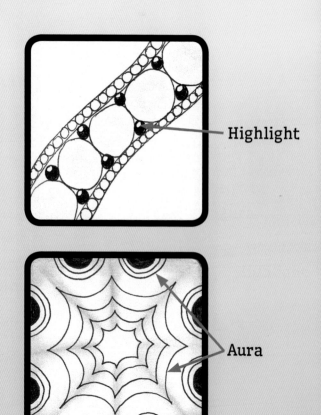

Highlight

Aura

# Essential Tangles

Here are some fantastic tangles to get you started! You can practice drawing each tangle on a square tile (see step 1 on page 18 for instructions). Each project in this book has a tangle key that tells you where to find the instructions for the tangles that have been used.

## Tipple

**1.** Start by drawing a small circle on your paper.

**2.** Add a few more circles around the first one. They can be any size you like.

**3.** Keep drawing circles of different sizes until the chosen space is full.

**4.** Shade in the spaces between the circles to finish your tangle.

# Bales

**1.** Draw evenly-spaced **diagonal** lines across the paper.

**2.** Draw diagonal lines in the opposite direction to make a **grid**.

**3.** Draw bumps along the bottom of all of the lines you drew in step 1.

**4.** Then draw bumps along the top of these lines.

 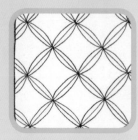

**5.** Repeat steps 3 and 4 on the diagonal lines that you drew in step 2.

**6.** Your pretty tangle is finished.

# Keeko

**1.** Draw four **horizontal** lines next to each other. They should be the same length and equally spaced apart.

**2.** Draw another four lines next to the first set, but this time make the lines **vertical**.

**3.** Repeat steps 1 and 2 until the row is complete.

**4.** Underneath each set of four horizontal lines, draw a set of four vertical lines.

**5.** Draw a set of four horizontal lines underneath each set of vertical lines.

**6.** Fill the chosen area, and then add some shading to finish it.

# Cadent

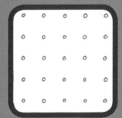 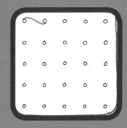 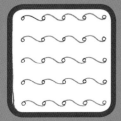  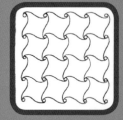

**1.** Draw a grid made up of small circles.

**2.** Draw a curve from the top of the first circle to the bottom of the second circle.

**3.** Repeat this pattern across each horizontal row of circles.

**4.** Now, use the same pattern to join up the vertical lines of circles.

**5.** Your Cadent tangle is complete.

# 'Nzeppel

 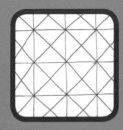 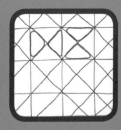  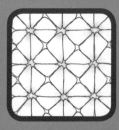

**1.** Draw horizontal and vertical lines over the paper to make a grid.

**2.** Now draw diagonal lines in both directions over the paper. They should be evenly spaced so they run through the middle of each square in the grid.

**3.** Each square in the grid should now be split into four triangular sections. Draw around the shape of each triangle, but round off the corners to create this pebble-like effect.

**4.** Continue to fill each square with triangles, as shown.

**5.** Add some shading to finish your tangle.

# Printemps

This tangle is perfect for creating swirly **textures**.

**1.** Draw a dot in the middle of your page. Then begin to draw a small **spiral** starting from the dot.

**2.** Continue drawing your spiral. You can make it as small or as big as you like.

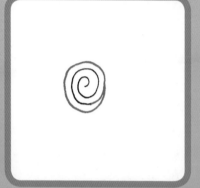

**3.** Once the spiral is the size that you want, turn the line in to close up the shape. You should have a smooth circle around the edge.

**4.** Add more spiral shapes around the first one.

**5.** Continue drawing Printemps spirals until you have filled the space.

# Fife

This woven mass of pretty petals brings
a floral touch to any picture.

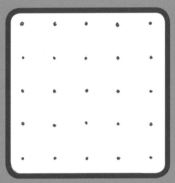

**1.** Start by drawing a grid of dots, like this.

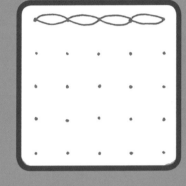

**2.** Draw a string of petals across the top row, using the dots as a guide.

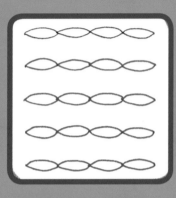

**3.** Repeat with a string of petals on each row.

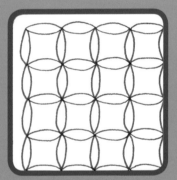

**4.** Now add vertical strings of petals to make a grid of overlapping circles.

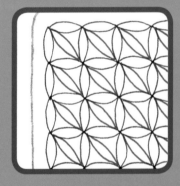

**5.** Inside each circle there is a bendy square. Add a petal inside each one, stretching from the top left to the bottom right.

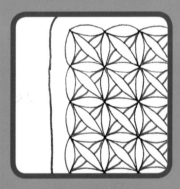

**6.** Now draw petals going in the opposite direction inside each square. When you meet a petal, stop the line and continue it on the other side.

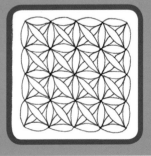

**7.** Your tangle is ready. You could add lines to the middle of each flower for extra twinkles.

# Beelight

### Make your birds really stand out with this eye-catching tangle.

**1.** Draw evenly-spaced vertical lines over the page.

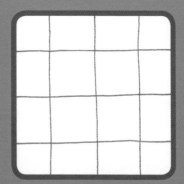

**2.** Add the same number of horizontal lines to make a grid of squares.

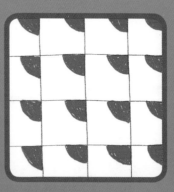

**3.** Draw a quarter of a circle in the top right-hand corner of each square and then fill them in with a pen.

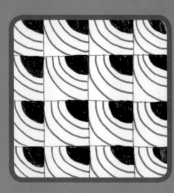

**4.** Add curved lines around each quarter circle to fill every square.

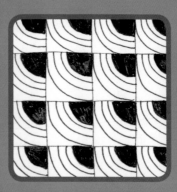

**5.** Your Beelight tangle is complete.

## Tangle Tip!

Leave a small "highlight" between a few of the curved lines to give Beelight some texture. Look at the swan's feathers on page 23.

# Tagh

**This tangle creates a lovely feathery effect, so it's perfect for a bird ZIA!**

**1.** Start by drawing a petal shape in the bottom left-hand corner of the shape.

**2.** Add another petal on either side of the first one.

**3.** Draw a row of narrow bumps above the petals. Begin and end each line in the middle of the shape in the row below.

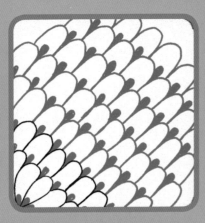

**4.** Carry on drawing more rows of bumps to fill the area. Then draw a small petal in the gap at the bottom of each shape and fill them in with your pen.

**5.** Your Tagh tangle is finished!

## Tangle Tip!
You could use this tangle on all sorts of bird pictures. It would also make great scales for reptiles!

# Shattuck

The overlapping layers in Shattuck create a striking effect on wings and tail feathers.

**1.** Draw three pairs of wavy lines, as shown, to make bands. Space the bands evenly across the paper.

**2.** Then draw several lines in the big space between two wavy lines.

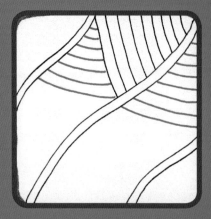

**3.** Draw several lines going in the opposite direction below the first set of lines. Add a set of lines between the next pair of bands.

**4.** Continue adding more sets of lines, changing direction each time until the area is full.

**5.** Add some pencil shading along the edges of each section to finish the tangle.

# Florz

**Combine this simple tangle with more elaborate ones for a really striking effect.**

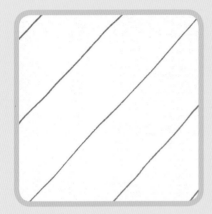

**1.** Start by drawing evenly-spaced diagonal lines across the paper.

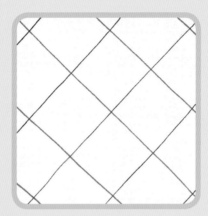

**2.** Now draw diagonal lines going in the opposite direction.

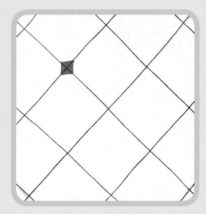

**3.** Draw a small square on a point where two lines cross. Fill in the square with a pen.

**4.** Continue adding squares and filling them in.

**5.** Your tangle is finished!

## Tangle Tip!

There are lots of ways you can be creative with this tangle. Try drawing a different shape where the lines cross, or using vertical lines for the grid.

# Crezn't

**This lovely looping tangle works equally well for a fish's scales or a bird's feathers.**

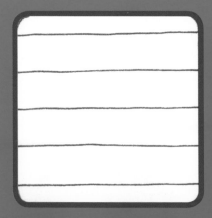

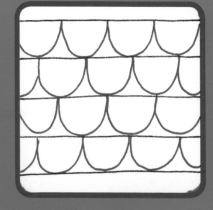

**1.** Draw horizontal lines across the paper.

**2.** Draw a string of "U" shapes between the top two lines. Draw more "U" shapes in the rows below. Begin and end each "U" in the middle of a "U" in the row above.

**3.** Add a smaller "U" inside each big "U," making sure the lines meet at the top.

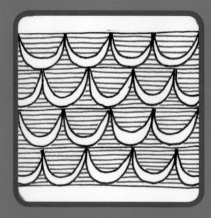

**4.** Draw evenly spaced horizontal lines in the spaces above and below the "U" shapes to create rows of little crescents.

**5.** Your tangle is ready!

# Gingham

**This tangle creates a simple but bold effect.**

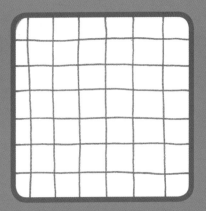

**1.** Start by drawing an odd number of evenly-spaced vertical and horizontal lines across the paper to make a grid.

**2.** Now use your pen to fill in every other square in every other row.

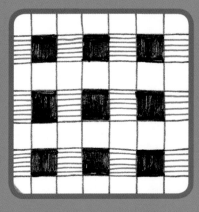

**3.** In the horizontal rows with filled in squares, fill the remaining blank squares with tightly-packed horizontal lines.

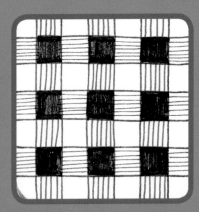

**4.** On the vertical rows with filled-in squares, draw tightly-packed vertical lines in the blank squares.

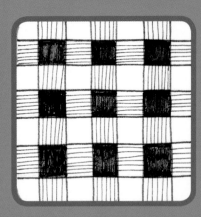

**5.** Your pretty checked pattern is complete!

# Onamato

The pearly strings in this tangle add sparkle and shine to make every picture feel precious.

**1.** Start by drawing two pairs of lines to make bands. Make sure you leave a wide gap between them.

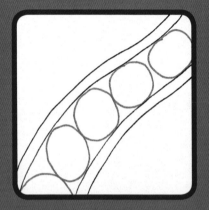

**2.** Draw tightly packed circles in between the bands. The circles should meet the lines at the top and bottom.

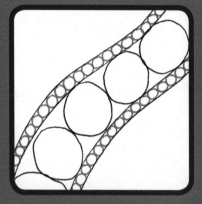

**3.** Fill the area inside each band with small, tightly-packed circles.

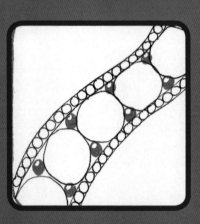

**4.** Draw small circles in the gaps between the big circles and fill them in, leaving a small highlight.

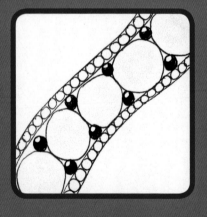

**5.** You could shade the big circles to make them look like they are catching the light.

## Tangle Tip!
This beautiful, simple tangle is a great way to add detail to tail feathers and wings.

# Strings, Tangles, and ZIAs

The Zentangle® method begins with drawing "strings." These are pencil lines that separate spaces inside a shape. The spaces are then filled with tangles to create your ZIA. Each project in this book starts with an outline of an animal with the strings already drawn in.

These steps show you how to build up a set of Zentangle® patterns on a Zentangle® tile. Tiles are good for practicing the tangles you've just learned. They can also be works of art themselves!

**1.** To create a square tile, use a ruler and pencil to draw four evenly-spaced dots for the corners. Connect the dots with straight lines.

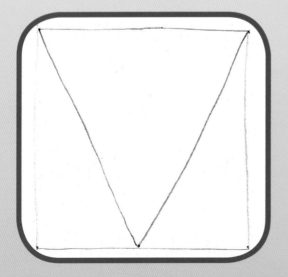

**2.** Now add strings to divide up the square. Draw a dot in the center of the bottom line. Then draw strings from the top corners to the new dot. This will create three triangle shapes to fill with tangles.

**3.** Choose a section to fill and a tangle to start with. We've chosen Printemps (page 9). Starting in one corner and using a pen, carefully fill the area with the tangle.

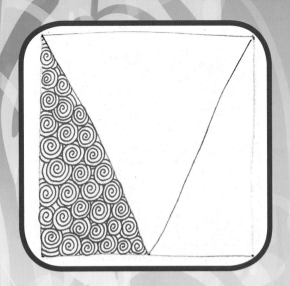

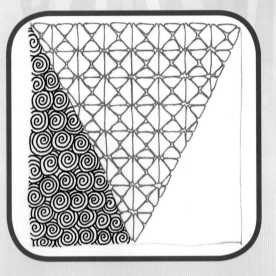

**4.** Now move to the next space created by the string. We've chosen to fill this section with 'Nzeppel (page 8).

**5.** In the final space, we've used Bales (page 7).

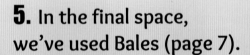

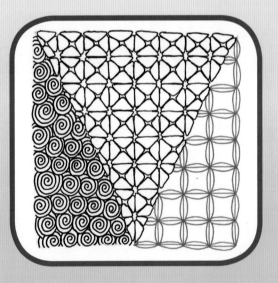

**6.** To complete the tangles, add shading to create shape and texture.

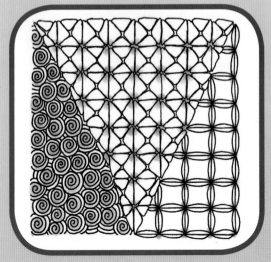

## Now you're ready to start your own tangles!

# Perfect Penguin

With their white tummies and black feathers, penguins look like they're wearing fancy tuxedoes! Follow these steps to give a plain penguin a stylish new look.

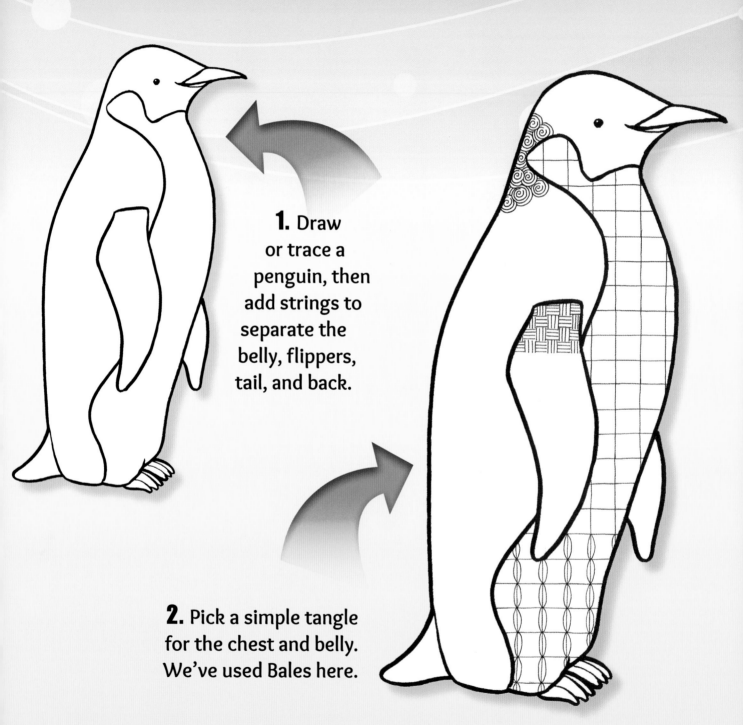

**1.** Draw or trace a penguin, then add strings to separate the belly, flippers, tail, and back.

**2.** Pick a simple tangle for the chest and belly. We've used Bales here.

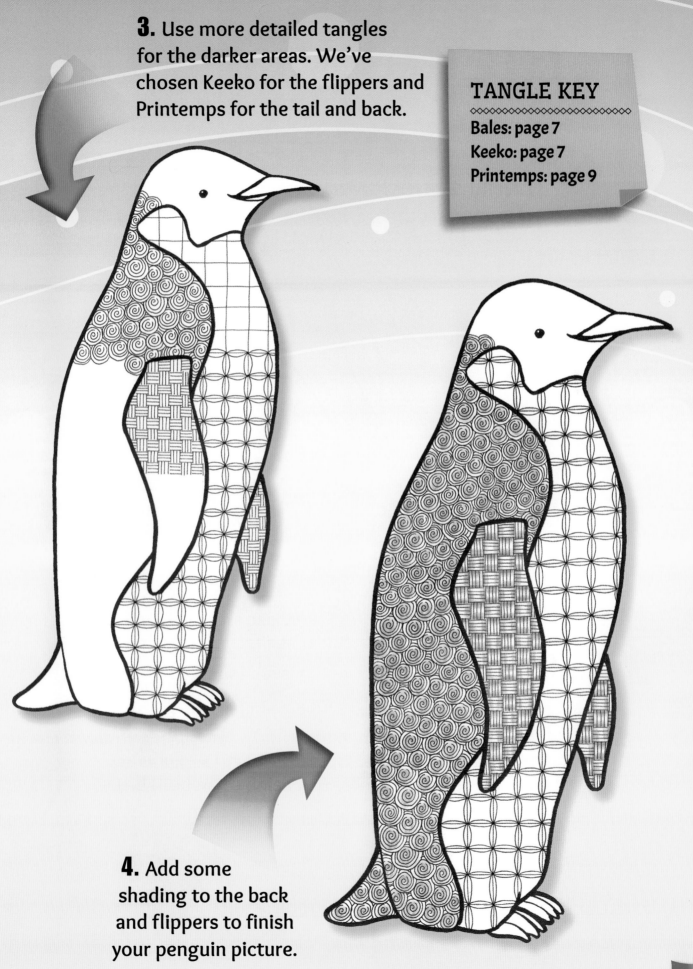

**3.** Use more detailed tangles for the darker areas. We've chosen Keeko for the flippers and Printemps for the tail and back.

**TANGLE KEY**
Bales: page 7
Keeko: page 7
Printemps: page 9

**4.** Add some shading to the back and flippers to finish your penguin picture.

# Elegant Swan

Swans glide effortlessly through the water with their elegant necks held high. You can create your own graceful Zentangle® swan in four simple steps.

**1.** Start by drawing or tracing the swan outline. Divide the wings into sections with curvy strings.

**2.** Begin to fill the wing sections with tangles. We've used Bales, Fife, and Beelight.

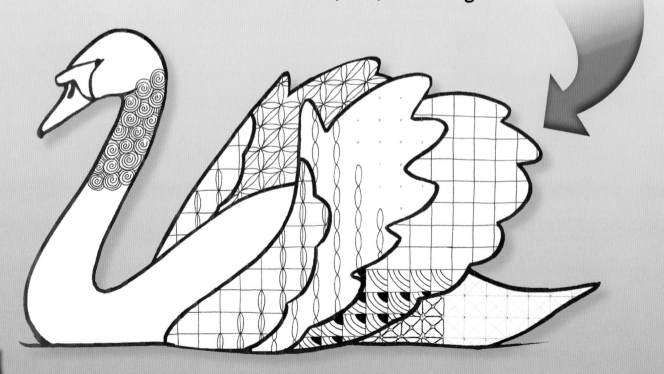

**3.** Continue tangling to complete the swan. We've chosen Printemps to represent the fluffy feathers on the neck and 'Nzeppel for the tail.

**TANGLE KEY**

Bales: page 7
Beelight: page 11
Fife: page 10
Printemps: page 9
'Nzeppel: page 8

**4.** Shade with a pencil on the neck and tail, and smudge with your finger to finish.

# Magical Owl

Owls swoop silently through the darkness, gliding on their wide, outstretched wings. Draw your own awesome owl with a fine set of tangled feathers.

**1.** Carefully draw or trace the owl outline and then add some strings along the wings.

**2.** Start to fill the wings with tangles. We've chosen Florz and Cadent for the main sections and Printemps for the wing tips.

## TANGLE KEY

Cadent: page 8

Florz: page 14

Printemps: page 9

Shattuck: page 13

Tagh: page 12

**3.** Pick tangles that give a nice feathery effect. We've used Tagh on the owl's chest and Shattuck on the tail.

**4.** Leave the face untangled so that the eyes really pop. Add shading on the wing tips and tail to finish your picture.

# Delicate Hummingbird

Tiny hummingbirds flash their bright feathers as they hover, collecting sweet nectar from flowers. Follow these steps to create a hummingbird covered in tangles from its beak to its tail.

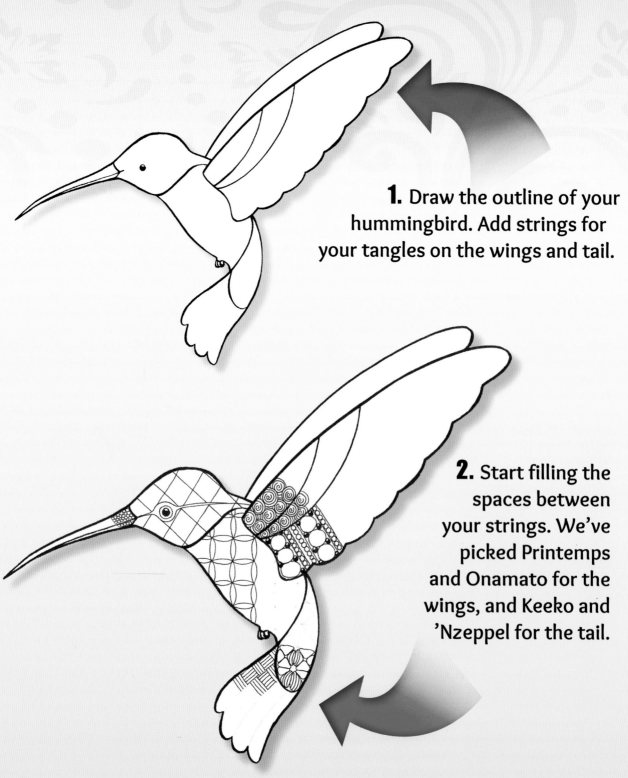

**1.** Draw the outline of your hummingbird. Add strings for your tangles on the wings and tail.

**2.** Start filling the spaces between your strings. We've picked Printemps and Onamato for the wings, and Keeko and 'Nzeppel for the tail.

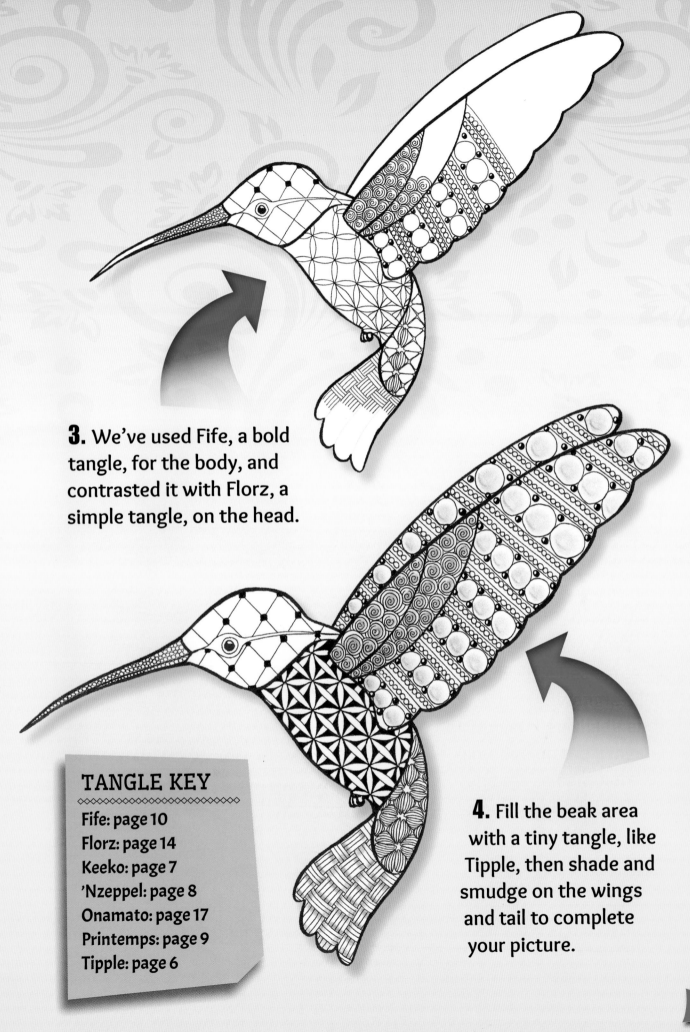

**3.** We've used Fife, a bold tangle, for the body, and contrasted it with Florz, a simple tangle, on the head.

## TANGLE KEY

Fife: page 10
Florz: page 14
Keeko: page 7
'Nzeppel: page 8
Onamato: page 17
Printemps: page 9
Tipple: page 6

**4.** Fill the beak area with a tiny tangle, like Tipple, then shade and smudge on the wings and tail to complete your picture.

# Pretty Parrot

Parrots' bright feathers and loud squawks make them easy to find in the leafy jungles where they live. Pick the perfect tangles for your parrot and it will really attract attention!

**1.** Draw or trace the outline of a parrot sitting on a branch. Add some wavy lines along the wing.

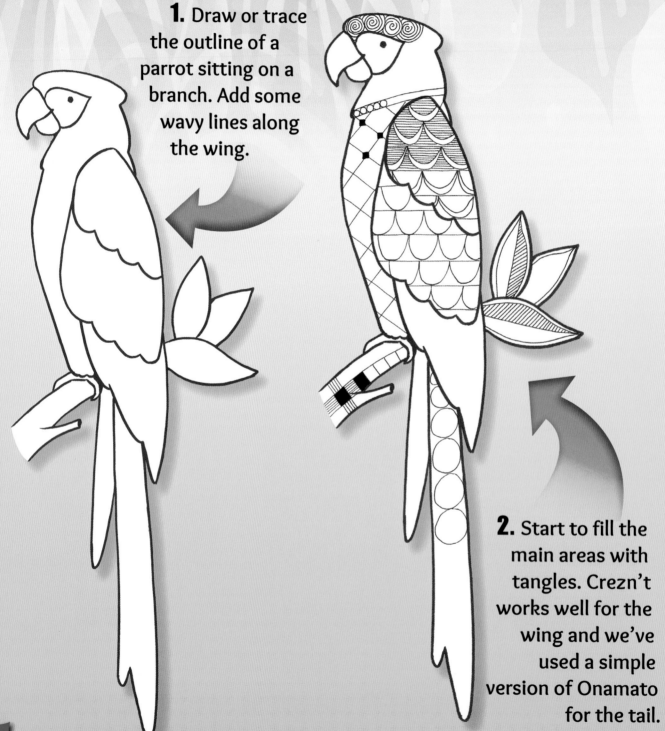

**2.** Start to fill the main areas with tangles. Crezn't works well for the wing and we've used a simple version of Onamato for the tail.

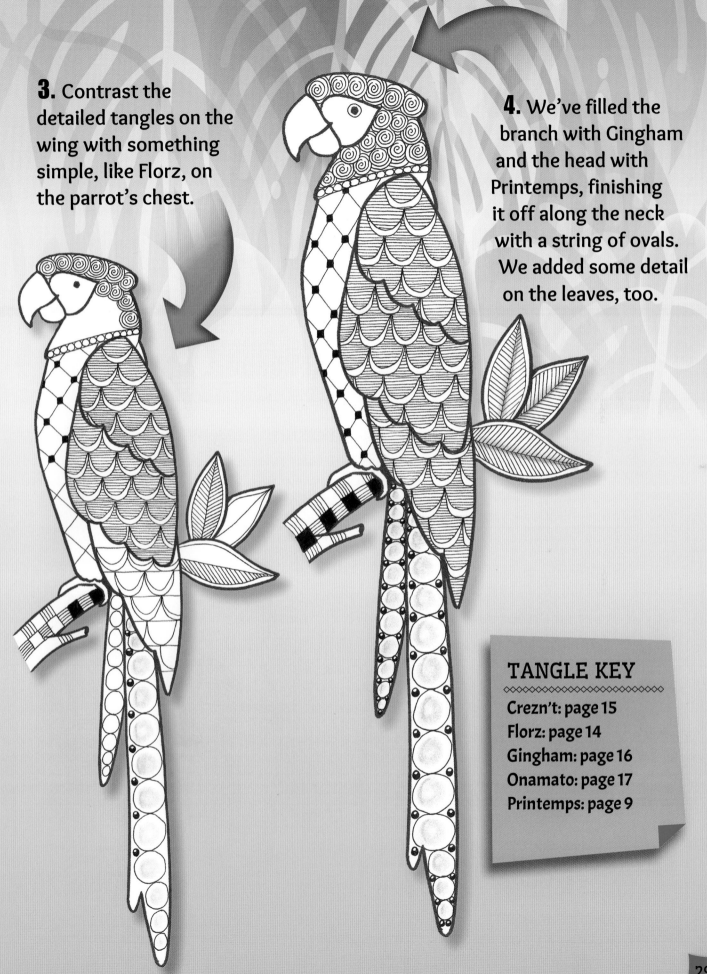

**3.** Contrast the detailed tangles on the wing with something simple, like Florz, on the parrot's chest.

**4.** We've filled the branch with Gingham and the head with Printemps, finishing it off along the neck with a string of ovals. We added some detail on the leaves, too.

## TANGLE KEY

Crezn't: page 15
Florz: page 14
Gingham: page 16
Onamato: page 17
Printemps: page 9

# Glossary

**beak** The hard mouthpart of a bird that sticks out from the face.

**contrast** To be strikingly different from something else.

**diagonal** A straight line at an angle.

**elaborate** Decorated with lots of detail.

**elegant** Beautiful and refined in shape or look.

**flipper** A wide, flat limb that is used for swimming.

**floral** Relating to flowers.

**grid** A set of uniform squares made from straight lines or points.

**horizontal** A straight line that is parallel to the horizon, the imaginary line where the ground meets the sky.

**hover** To stay in one place in the air.

**jungle** An area of thick, tropical forest.

**nectar** A sweet substance produced by flowers to encourage bees and other insects to feed from them.

**pattern** A set of shapes or a design that is repeated.

**spiral** A shape made from a line moving outwards in a circular pattern from a central point.

**texture** The look or feel of a surface.

**vertical** A line or object that stands straight up, at right angles with the horizon.

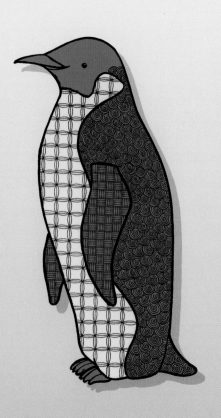

# Further Information

## Books to Read

***100 Birds to Fold and Fly***
Emily Bone
Usborne Publishing, 2016

***Zentangle® for Kids***
Jane Marbaix
Sterling Children's Books, 2015

***Zentangle® for Kids: With Tangles, Templates and Pages to Tangle On***
Beate Winkler
Quarry Books, 2016

## Websites

Check out this awesome website for bird coloring pages!
**www.supercoloring.com/coloring-pages/birds**

Find out more about Zentangle® at the official website.
**https://www.zentangle.com**

Learn new tangles at this fun site!
**http://tanglepatterns.com**

**Publisher's note to educators and parents:** Our editors have carefully reviewed these websites to ensure that they are suitable for students. Many websites change frequently, however, and we cannot guarantee that a site's future contents will continue to meet our high standards of quality and educational value. Be advised that students should be closely supervised whenever they access the Internet.

# Index